LYNN REISER

BEACH FEET

GREENWILLOW BOOKS, NEW YORK

T H E
FRIENDS
of the
Beverly Hills
Public Library

Watercolor paints and a black pen were used for the full-color art. The text type is Swiss 721 BT.

Printed in Hong Kong by South China Printing Company (1988) Ltd.
First Edition
10 9 8 7 6 5 4 3 2 1

LIBRARY OF CONGRESS CATALOGING-IN-PUBLICATION DATA

Reiser, Lynn.
Beach feet / by Lynn Reiser.
 p.   cm.
Summary: The beach displays human feet which squish, splash, or rest, as well as animal feet which may number five, six, or even nine and which have many uses.
ISBN 0-688-14400-4 (trade).   ISBN 0-688-14401-2 (lib. bdg.)
[1. Foot—Fiction.   2. Beaches—Fiction.   3. Animals—Fiction.]   I. Title.
PZ7.R27745Bal   1996   [E]—dc20   95-12208   CIP   AC

THANK-YOU NOTES

 To Laurita, Walker, Judy, and John
for feet.

 To Pica and Cinnamon
for paws.

 To Zöe and Chris
for shoes.

 To Sanibel Island
for shells.

 To Morton, Susan, Suzy, John and
Ward, Chris and Esther, Betsy, Susie,
Kate, Kay, and Phyllis
for reading and reading.

 To José H. Leal, Ph.D.,
Rosenstiel School of Marine and Atmospheric
Science, University of Miami, Miami, Florida,
and
Nancy Rosenbaum, M.S.,
Department of Biology, Yale University,
New Haven, Connecticut, and Children's School
of Science, Woods Hole, Massachusetts,
for reviewing beach facts.

And

 To Susan and Ava,
always.

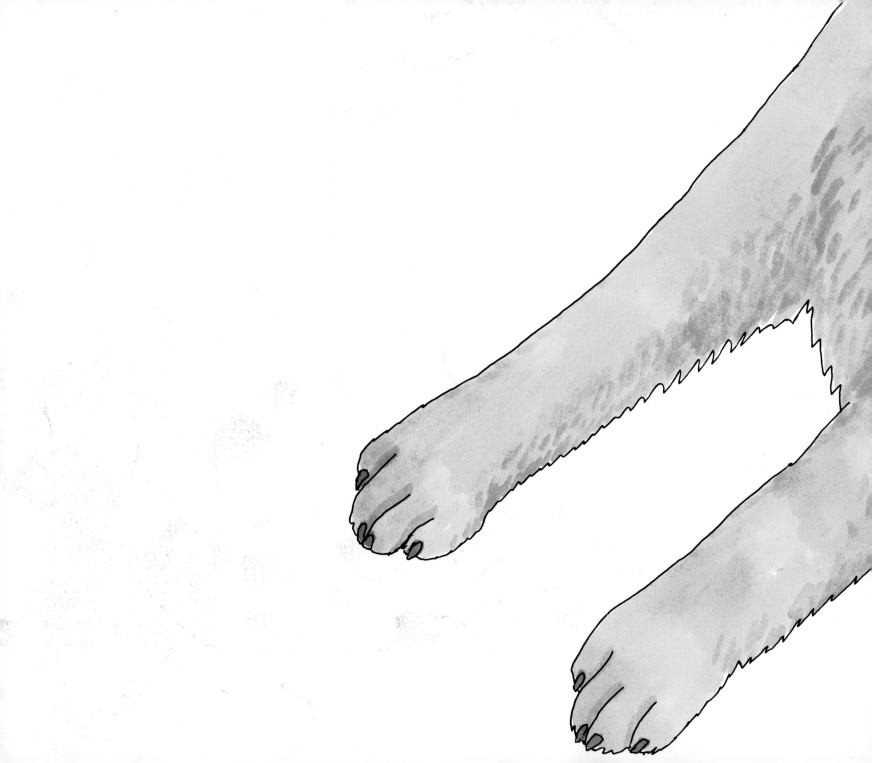

Hello, feet.

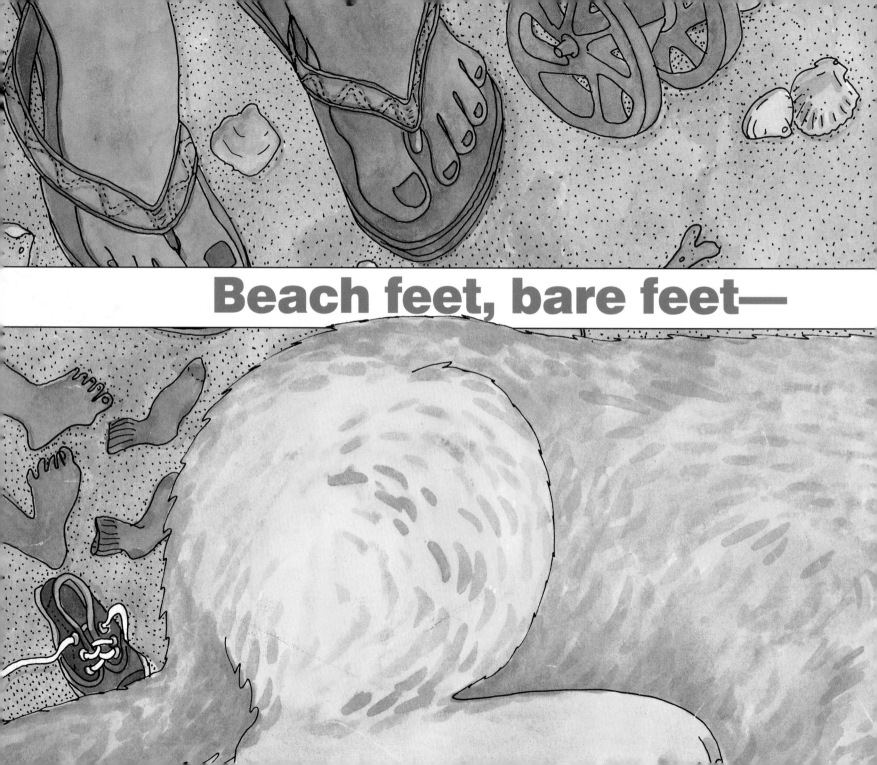

Beach feet, bare feet—

look at my feet.

Dry hot red feet,

 FOOTNOTE

Hot sun
and hot sand
make feet feel hot
and look red.

wet cold blue feet.

 FOOTNOTE
The reflection
of the blue sky
can make the water
and the feet in it
look blue.
Cold water
makes feet feel cold
and look blue.

Scrunch feet,

 FOOTNOTE
A shell breaks into sand when feet and waves scrunch it into tiny pieces.

squash feet,

 FOOTNOTE
An air bladder on the sargassum seaweed (*Sargassum*) pops when feet or teeth squash it.

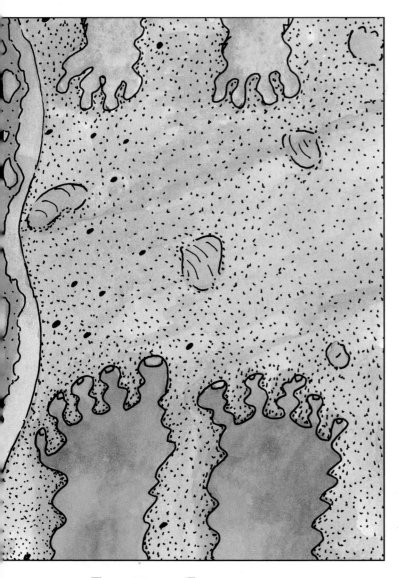

squish feet,

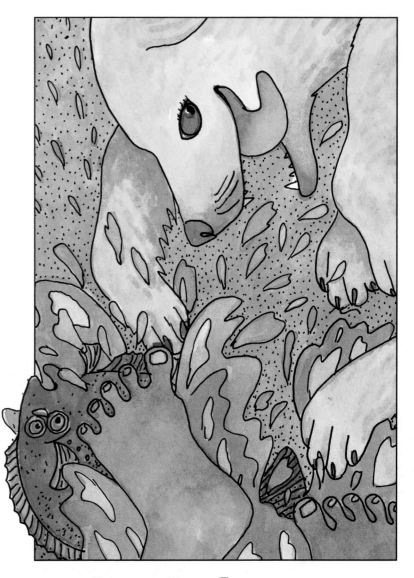

splash feet,

FOOTNOTE
Splashing feet can frighten a flounder (*Paralichthys*) buried in the sand.

ride feet, rest feet—

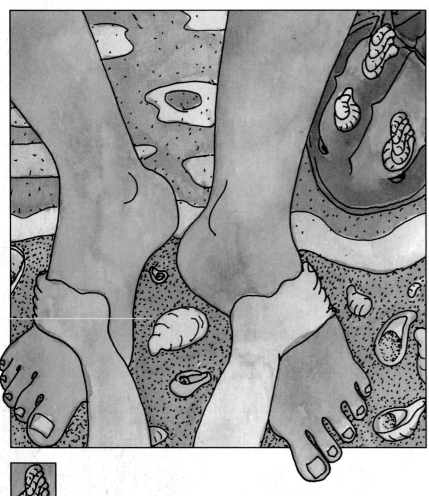

FOOTNOTE

A whelk (*Busycon*)
can pull its foot and head
into its shell
to rest.
It blocks the opening
with a horn-like disk
called the operculum.

FOOTNOTE

A hermit crab (*Pagurus*)
can pull its feet and head
into its borrowed shell
to rest.
It blocks the opening
with its big front claws.

FOOTNOTE

A slippersnail (*Crepidula*)
lives in a stack of slippersnails.
It holds on with its foot.
The stack rides
on another animal's shell.

stop and count feet.

One,

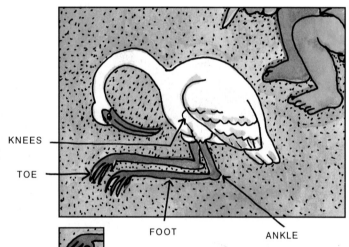

KNEES

TOE

FOOT

ANKLE

two,

three feet,

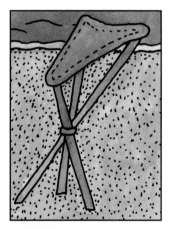

FOOTNOTE

A clam (*Mercenaria*)
uses its one foot
to burrow deep
into the sand.

FOOTNOTE

The bones in the two feet
of an ibis (*Eudocimus*)
are toe bones.
The bones in its scaly legs
are foot bones.
Its "knees" look backward
because they are ankle bones.

FOOTNOTE

A stool can
stand alone
on three feet.

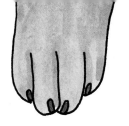

four,

 FOOTNOTE

raccoon (*Procyon*)
ses its feet
catch crabs
nd clams.

five,

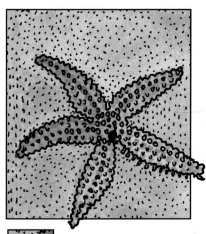

 FOOTNOTE

The real feet of the
Forbes sea star (*Asterias*)
are the little tube feet
along each of
its five rays.

six feet,

 FOOTNOTE

A fly (*Tabanus*)
has six feet.

seven feet,

FOOTNOTE
A seagull (*Larus*)
faces into the wind and
tucks up one foot to rest.

eight feet, nine feet, no feet.

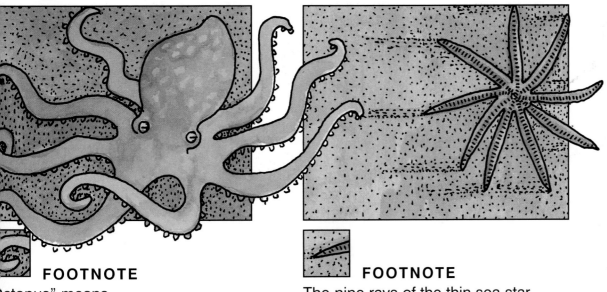

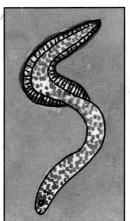

FOOTNOTE
"octopus" means
"eight feet" in Greek.

FOOTNOTE
The nine rays of the thin sea star
(*Asterias*) break off easily.
Then the thin sea star can grow
a new ray.

NOTE
The eel (*Gymnothorax*)
has no feet. It swims
by bending its body.

Slimy, salty, sandy feet,

 FOOTNOTE

The moonsnail (*Polinices*)
uses a fold of its wide foot
to cover its head
as it plows blindly
through the sand.

 FOOTNOTE

A sand dollar (*Mellita*)
hides just under the sand
and pokes tiny feet
up for oxygen and
to move food to its mouth.

 FOOTNOTE

A sand fly (*Phlebotomus*)
tastes with its feet.

 FOOTNOTE

Salt in seawater makes
beach feet taste like salt.

 FOOTNOTE

A periwinkle snail (*Littorina*)
puts a carpet of slime
under its foot to smooth
its way over rough rocks.

FOOTNOTE

The shell of
an angel's toenail
(*Anomia*) gleams
silver, pink, or gold.

FOOTNOTE

A snowy egret (*Egretta*)
has bright yellow feet.
Other egrets have
black feet.

FOOTNOTE

A male fiddler crab (*Uca*)
holds its big claw
like a fiddle.

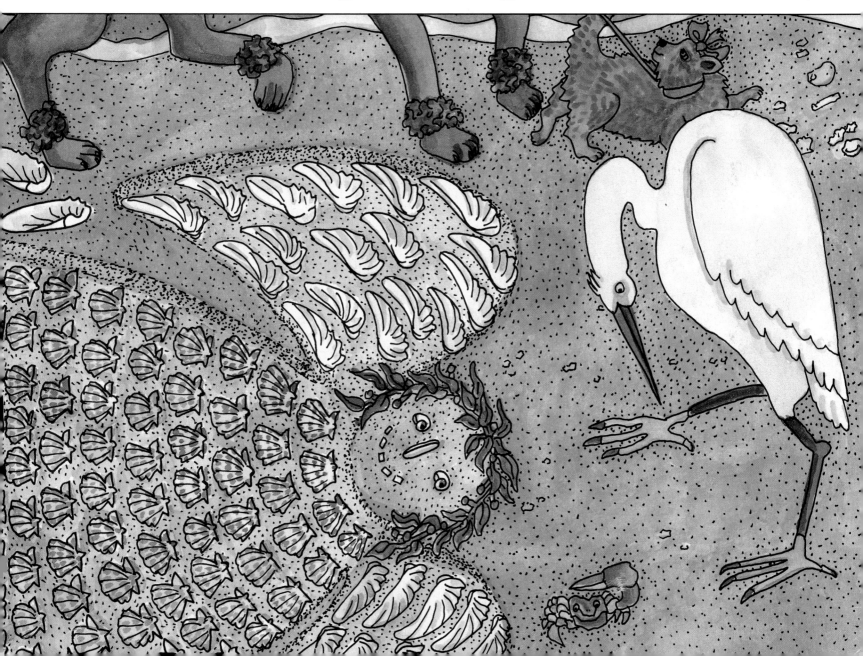

furry, fancy, fiddle feet,

claw feet, paw feet,

FOOTNOTE

The clawed foot of an osprey (*Pandion*) has four toes: two in front, one in back, and one that can move from front to back in order to hold its catch.

FOOTNOTE

A gopher tortoise (*Gopherus*) uses its claws to dig giant burrows.

FOOTNOTE

A hermit crab (*Pagurus*) uses its hard front claws to fight and walk and eat. Its soft back claws clutch its shell.

FOOTNOTE

The feet of a dog (*Canis*) sweat when it is hot or worried.

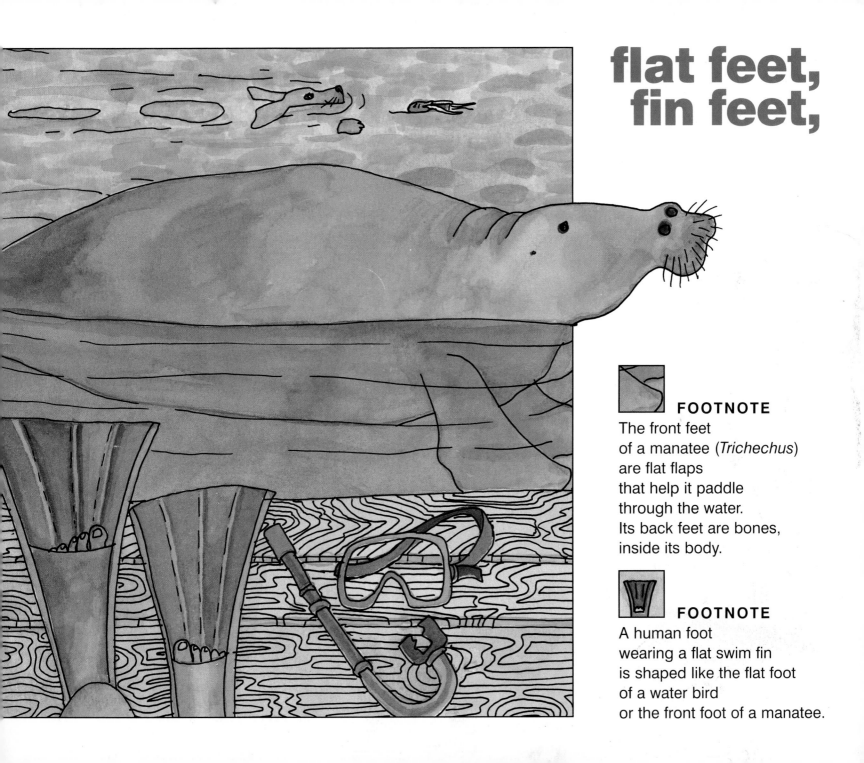

flat feet, fin feet,

FOOTNOTE

The front feet
of a manatee (*Trichechus*)
are flat flaps
that help it paddle
through the water.
Its back feet are bones,
inside its body.

FOOTNOTE

A human foot
wearing a flat swim fin
is shaped like the flat foot
of a water bird
or the front foot of a manatee.

upside-down feet,

FOOTNOTE

A barnacle (*Balanus*)
lies on its back in its shell
and kicks its fringed feet
up into the water
to net food floating by.

FOOTNOTE

If it turns upside down,
a horseshoe crab (*Limulus*)
uses its hard tail to flip
its shell right side up.
Then it stands on its ten fee

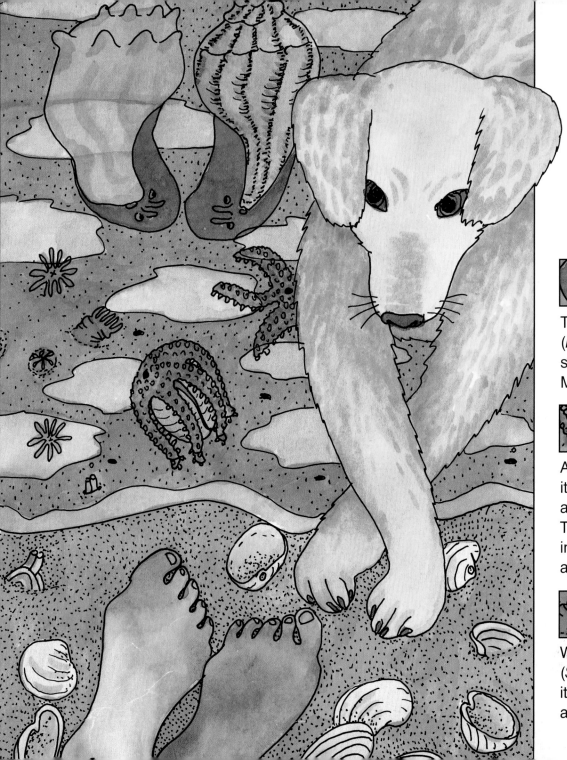

FOOTNOTE

The foot of the lightning whelk
(*Busycon contrarium*)
spirals out of its shell to the left.
Most whelks' feet spiral to the right.

FOOTNOTE

A sea star (*Asterias*) attaches
its feet outside a clam's shell
and very slowly pulls it open.
Then it slips its stomach
into the shell
and digests the clam.

FOOTNOTE

When a burrowing anemone
(*Sagartia*) is disturbed,
it pulls in its tentacle feet
and squeezes into the sand.

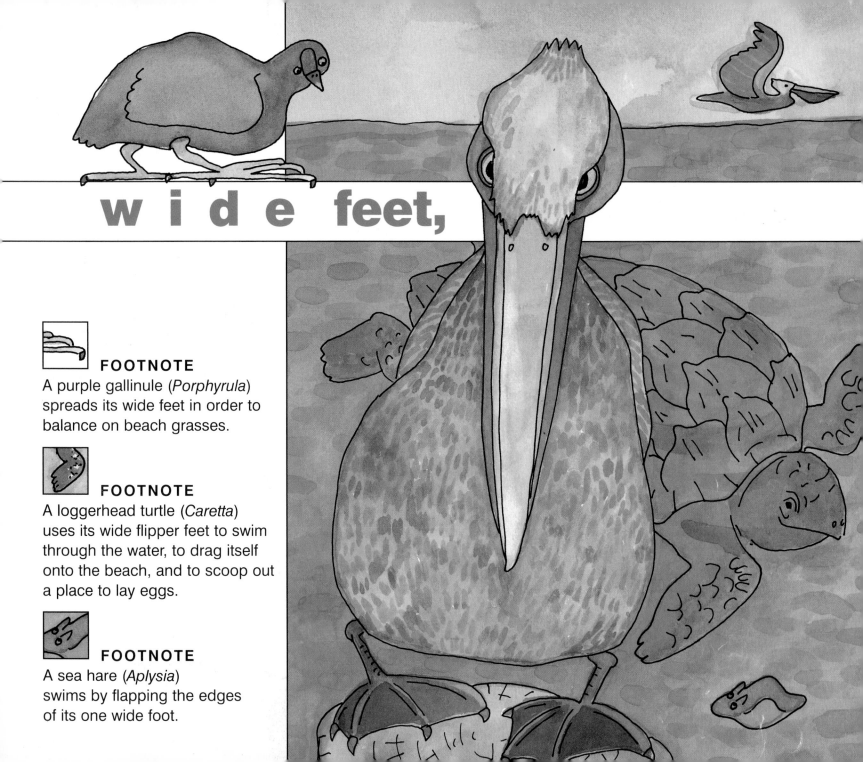

w i d e feet,

FOOTNOTE

A purple gallinule (*Porphyrula*) spreads its wide feet in order to balance on beach grasses.

FOOTNOTE

A loggerhead turtle (*Caretta*) uses its wide flipper feet to swim through the water, to drag itself onto the beach, and to scoop out a place to lay eggs.

FOOTNOTE

A sea hare (*Aplysia*) swims by flapping the edges of its one wide foot.

webbed feet.

FOOTNOTE
The wide feet of a pelican (*Pelecanus*) have webbing connecting all four toes. It uses its wide, webbed feet to speed takeoff and to slow landing.

FOOTNOTE
A dog (*Canis*) bred for working in water has wide webbed paws that help it swim.

FOOTNOTE
The webbed feet of a loon (*Gavia*) are set far back on its body. This helps it dive, but makes walking clumsy.

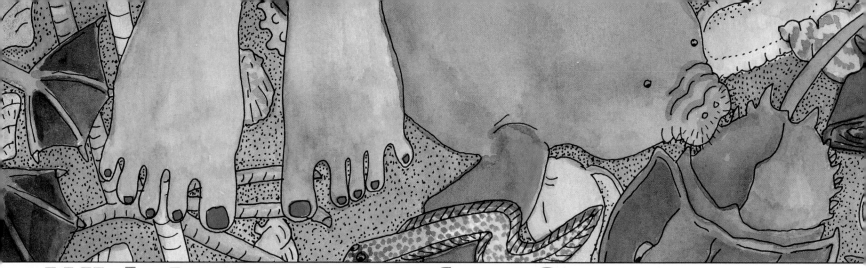

Which are your feet?

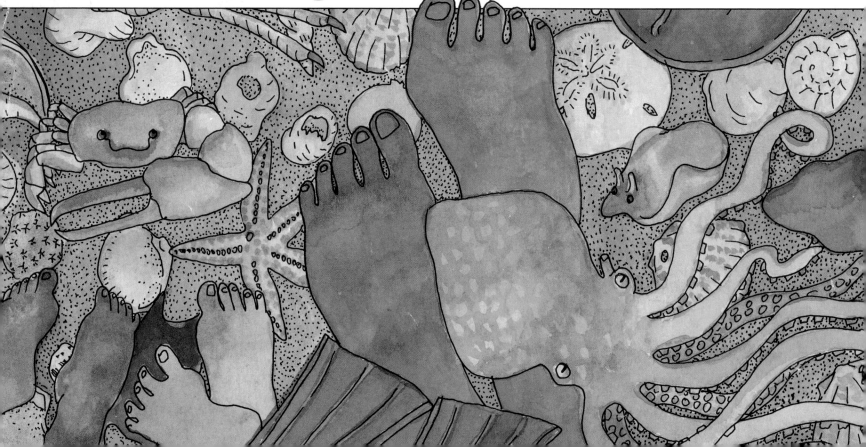

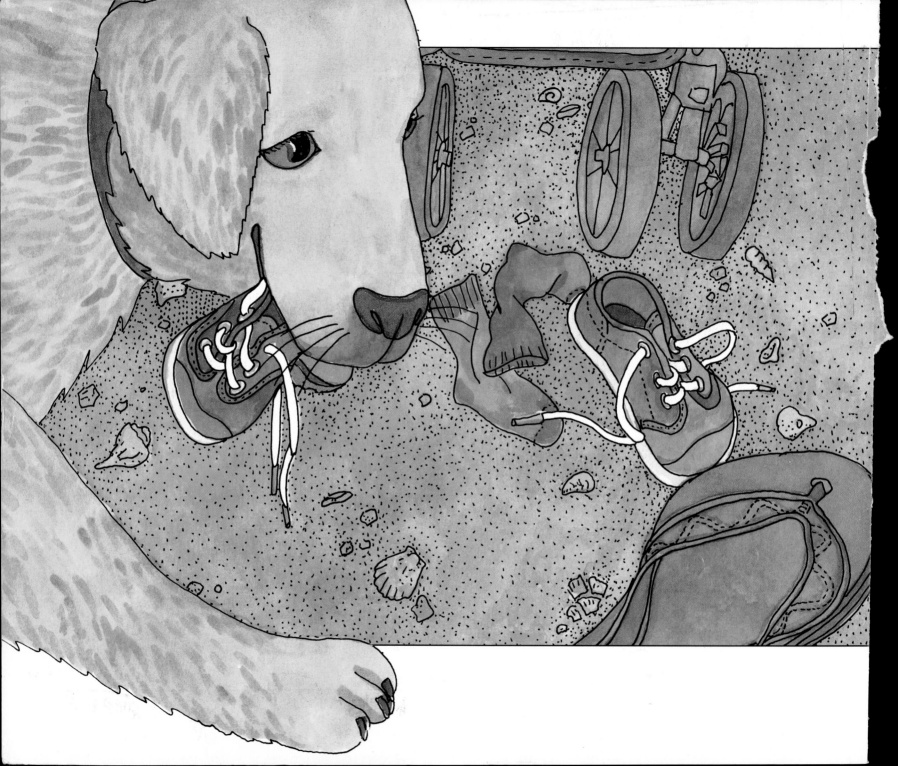

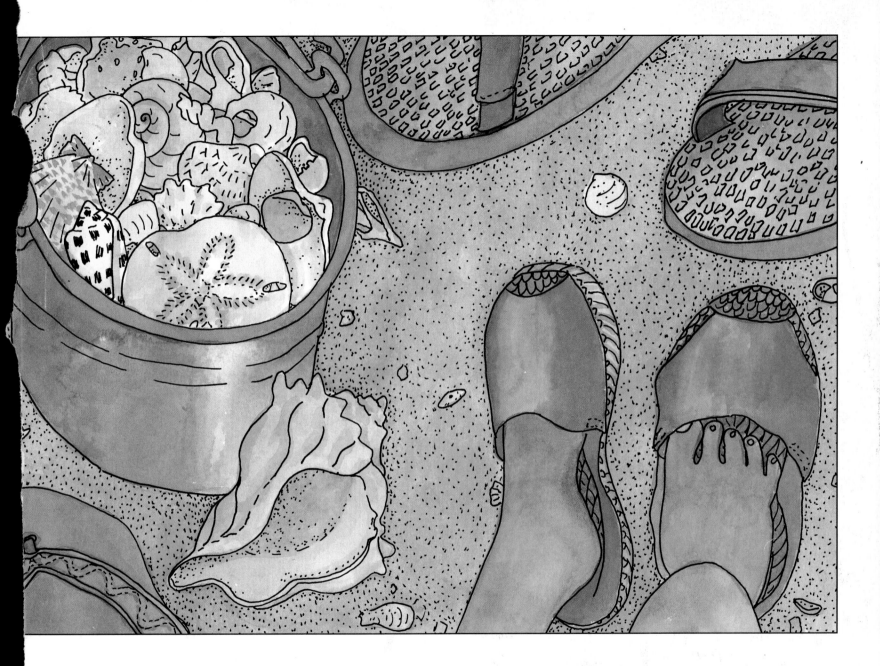

Good-bye, feet.

Feet repeat!

Hello, feet.
Beach feet, bare feet—
look at my feet.
Dry hot red feet,
wet cold blue feet.
Scrunch feet, squash feet,
squish feet, splash feet,
ride feet, rest feet—
stop and count feet.
One, two, three feet,
four, five, six feet,
seven feet, eight feet,
nine feet,
no feet.
Slimy, salty, sandy feet,
furry, fancy, fiddle feet,
claw feet, paw feet,
flat feet, fin feet,
upside-down feet,
outside-in feet,
wide feet, webbed feet.
Which are your feet?
Good-bye, feet.